This book belongs to ...

WITHDRAWN

....

TOPIC

Tips for Talking and Reading Together

Stories are an enjoyable and reassuring way of introducing children to new experiences.

Before you read the story:

- Talk about the title and the picture on the cover. Ask your child what they think the story might be about.
- Talk about what happens in a hospital. Has your child ever had to go to hospital? What do they remember about the experience?

Read the story with your child. After you have read the story:

- Discuss the Talk About ideas on page 27.
- Talk about the treatment for a broken leg on pages 28–29. Then talk about what might happen if you broke your arm.
- Do the fun activity on page 30.

Have fun!

Find the 10 stickers hidden in the pictures.

For more hints and tips on helping your child become a successful and enthusiastic reader look at our website www.oxfordowl.co.uk.

Going to the Hospital

Written by Roderick Hunt and Annemarie Young

Illustrated by Alex Brychta

OXFORD
UNIVERSITY PRESS

Chip was doing step-ups. He was training for
a football match that was on the next day.

4

"Look out!" said Craig. "Your shoelace is undone."
But it was too late.

Chip fell onto the bench. He yelled out in pain.
Dad came running over.

"My leg really hurts," said Chip. "I can't stand up."
"I think I'd better take you to the hospital," said Dad.

"Poor Chip," said Dad. "I'll phone Mum and get her to come and meet us."

Mum was waiting for them with a wheelchair. "You park the car and I'll check us in. Meet us in the waiting area," she told Dad.

A nurse took Chip and Mum to a cubicle. "Tell me what happened," said the nurse.

Chip told him how he had fallen, and showed him his leg.

"Look at this chart. Point to the picture to show me how bad the pain is," said the nurse. "I can give you some medicine for the pain."

"You need to have an X-ray so we can see if your bone is broken," said the nurse. "The porter will take you for a ride in the wheelchair."

"The X-ray machine takes a picture of the bone in your leg," said the radiographer. "It won't hurt."

"I know," said Chip. "It's OK."

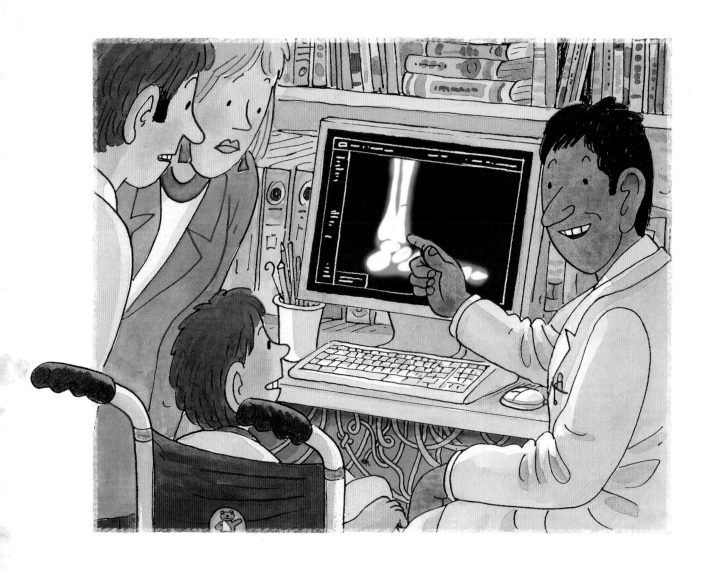

"You've cracked this bone in your leg," said the doctor. "We'll give you a plaster cast now. Then come back on Monday for the fracture clinic."

Mum helped hold Chip's leg while the plaster was put on.
"It will feel nice and warm," said the nurse.

"Don't put weight on your leg. Don't get the plaster wet, or poke anything down it!" said the nurse. "If it's sore, tell Mum or Dad."

The nurse gave Chip some crutches and showed him
how to use them.

"It's hard," said Chip.

"You're doing well," said Dad.

The next day, Chip and Craig watched the football game. "I wish I was playing," said Chip. "It's so exciting."

"I play basketball and that's just as exciting," said Craig.
"Want to watch me play next week?"

"Yes, please," said Chip.

On Monday, Mum took Chip to the fracture clinic at the hospital.

"The cracked bone will be better in about six weeks," said the doctor.

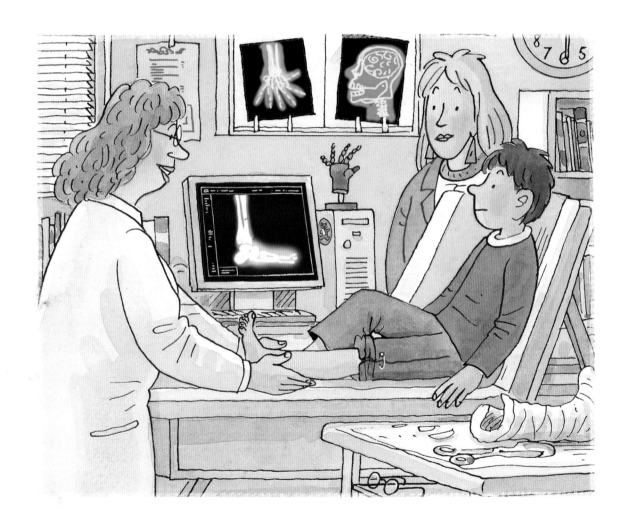

Chip got a new cast that he could walk on. "Can
I have a green one?" he asked. "It's the same colour
as my football team."

Chip showed Biff and Kipper his new cast. "Can I draw on it?" asked Kipper.

"No way," said Chip.

"Look out!" said Biff. "Don't trip over Floppy and break your arm too."

The next day, Dad took Chip to watch Craig play basketball.

"Wow," said Chip. "It's really exciting. I'd love to play too."

"I'll teach you when your leg is better," said Craig. "Let's go and play football now."

"You're really good at this," said Chip.
"I've had lots of practice!" said Craig.

Talk about the story

How did Chip hurt his leg?

Why did the radiographer take an X-ray?

How did Chip feel when he was watching the football match?

For what other reasons do children sometimes visit hospital?

If you go to hospital with a broken leg you ...

See a nurse

Have an X-ray

Have a plaster cast
put on your leg

Are given
crutches

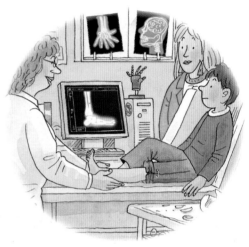

Go back to the
fracture clinic

Have a new,
light cast put on
your leg

What do you think happens if you break your arm?

Spot the pair

Find the two pictures of Chip that are exactly the same.

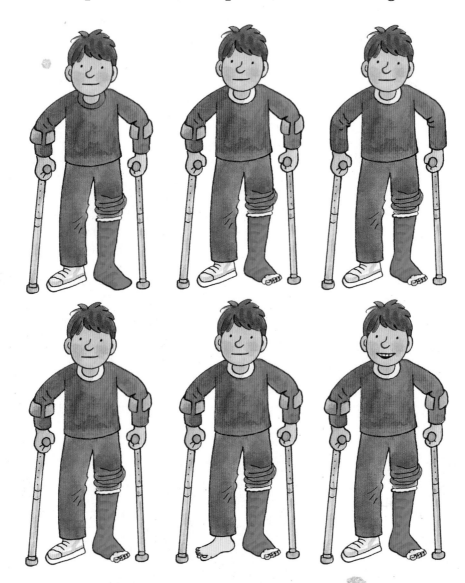

Have you read them all yet?

First Experiences with Biff, Chip & Kipper

Kipper's First Pet

Learning to Swim

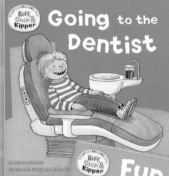

Going to the Dentist

Going to the Doctor

Going on a Plane

Going to the Hairdresser

Fun at the Farm

Starting School

FIRST EXPERIENCES Flashcards
55 cards

Also available:
- Kipper Gets Nits!
- Going to the Hospital
- Going to the Optician
- Let's Recycle!
- Going on a Train
- Going to the Vet
- Kipper's First Match
- Kipper's First Dance Class
- A New Baby!

Read with Biff, Chip and Kipper
The UK's best-selling home reading series

	Phonics	First Stories
Level 1 Getting ready to read		
Level 2 Starting to read		
Level 3 Becoming a reader		
Level 4 Developing as a reader		
Level 5 Building confidence in reading		
Level 6 Reading with confidence		

Phonics stories help children practise their sounds and letters, as they learn to do in school.

First stories have been specially written to provide practice in reading everyday language.

OXFORD
UNIVERSITY PRESS

Great Clarendon Street, Oxford OX2 6DP

Text © Roderick Hunt and Annemarie Young 2009
Illustrations © Alex Brychta 2009
First published 2009
This edition published 2014

10 9 8 7 6 5 4 3 2
Series Editors: Kate Ruttle, Annemarie Young
British Library Cataloguing in Publication Data available
ISBN: 978-0-19-273678-9
Printed in China by Imago
The characters in this work are the original creation of Roderick Hunt and Alex Brychta who retain copyright in the characters.
With thanks to Tessa Sharp BSc Hons, RGN, ENB 199, and Dr Veronica Spooner, MB BS MRCGP